THIS

READ with ME ™

BOOK
BELONGS TO

THIS BELONGS TO
JEREMY

Library of Congress Cataloging in Publication Data

Horowitz, Susan.
  Hansel and Gretel with Benjy and Bubbles.

  (Read With Me series)
  Based on the fairy tale by the Brothers Grimm.
  SUMMARY: A rhymed retelling of the classic tale
with Benjy the bunny and Bubbles the cat clarifying
values as the story unfolds.
  [1. Fairy tales. 2. Folklore—Germany.
3. Stories in rhyme] I. Razzi, James. II. Grimm,
Jakob Ludwig Karl, 1785-1863. Hänsel und Gretel.
III. Title. IV. Series.
PZ8.3.H785Han   398.2'2   [E]   77-28451
ISBN 0-03-040246-8

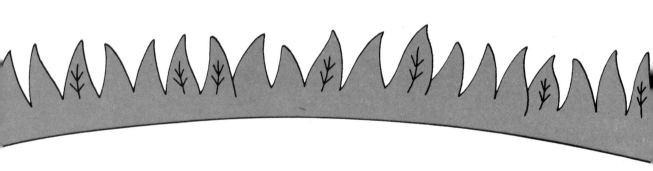

Hansel and Gretel
with Benjy and Bubbles

Adapted by SUSAN HOROWITZ

Illustrated by JIM RAZZI

Edited by RUTH LERNER PERLE

Holt, Rinehart and Winston   •   New York

Hansel and Gretel had a very hard life.
They lived with their father and his very mean wife.

One night, the children could not sleep.
They heard their father sigh and weep.
"Wife," he said, "what shall we do?
We have barely food for two."
The wife replied, "We can't feed four.
Without the children we'd have more!
Let us take them to the wood;
We can leave them there for good."

Hansel and Gretel had a poor father.
He had a mean wife. "Let us leave Hansel
and Gretel in the woods," she said.

When she heard the mean wife speak,
Tears ran down poor Gretel's cheek.
She cried, "How will we find our way
If they leave us there to stay?"

Benjy, the bunny, softly kissed her,
And Hansel said, "Don't cry, dear sister.
I have a plan that cannot fail—
We'll make a secret breadcrumb trail.
At every step we'll drop a crumb
So we can see which way we've come."

Hansel said, "We will find our way home.
We will make a trail with bits of bread."

Next day, the mean wife said, "Be good
And come with me into the wood."
"We'll come with you," the children said,
"If you give us a piece of bread."

Their father gave them all he could,
Then they started for the wood.
Benjy followed with a hop.
He saw the children turn and stop
And every time they turned around,
They dropped a breadcrumb on the ground.

The mean wife asked, "Why do you stop?"
They said, "To see our bunny hop."

Hansel and Gretel went into the woods.
They dropped bits of bread on the way.

When the woods grew thick and deep,
The wife said, "Children, go to sleep!
We'll be back in just a while."
Then, she smiled a nasty smile.

The sun went down, the sky turned black,
The grown-ups never did come back!

Hansel said, "Don't be afraid,
We'll find the trail the breadcrumbs made."
But when they looked, the crumbs weren't there!
Birds ate them all, the ground was bare!

They walked all night, till it was day;
Still, they could not find their way
Just trees and brush on every side —
"We're lost forever!" Hansel cried.

The birds ate all the bread bits.
Hansel and Gretel were lost!

But when Benjy hopped ahead,
They saw a house of gingerbread!
Rock candy made each window pane,
A cookie roof kept out the rain,
A chocolate chimney was on top,
The doorknob was a lollypop!

The children ran ahead in haste
To reach the house and have a taste.

As they were nibbling gingerbread,
From inside, a strange voice said,

"Nibble, nibble, little mouse,
Who's that nibbling at my house?"

In the woods, they saw a house.

The house was made of cookies and cake.

The cookie door then opened wide;
The strange voice said, "Do come inside!
You're tired and hungry, I can tell,
Although I cannot see too well.
Poor children, you're so pale and thin,
I'll give you sweets if you'll come in."

The children stepped inside the door
And saw a strange old crone who wore
A purple cloak and pointed hat.
And petted Bubbles, her mean cat.

An old woman said, "Come in."

She fed them cake and gingerbread
And tucked them in a little bed.
But all her kindness was a trap.
It was a *witch* who watched them nap!

While little Hansel lay in bed,
The witch crept up to him and said,
"Soon, you greedy little brat,
I'll lock you up and make you fat.
As soon as you are plump and nice
I'll brew you and stew you and chew you with rice!"

She woke him up and in a rage,
She locked poor Hansel in a cage!

The woman was a witch!
She put Hansel in a cage.

When Gretel woke, she cried in fright,
"Who locked my brother up so tight?"

"*I* locked him up!" the mean witch said.
"I'll feed him sausages and bread;
I'll make him eat up every crumb,
And every day, I'll pinch his thumb.
When Hansel's thumb gets plump and sweet,
I'll know he's fat enough to eat!"

The witch wanted to eat Hansel.
She wanted him to get nice and fat.

So, every day she gave a pinch
To see if Hansel grew an inch.
But Hansel fooled the blind old crone
And held out an old chicken bone.
She said, "How little you must weigh,
We'll fatten you just one more day."

The witch said, "Hold out your finger,
Hansel. I want to see if it is fat yet."
Hansel held out a bone.

One day, the witch, in a hungry rage,
Looked at Hansel in the cage.
She said, "I'm much too starved to wait;
My boy, we have a dinner date!
Gretel, chop some firewood,
Roasted Hansel will taste good!"

Gretel got down on her knees,
And begged, "Don't hurt my brother, *please*!"
The witch said with a nasty laugh,
"I'll eat you too, you silly calf!"

And Bubbles meowed, "I'm hungry, too.
Perhaps I'll have some bunny stew."

The witch said, "I am going
to cook Hansel!"

The witch made Gretel light the fire,
And as the flames leaped higher and higher,
The witch said, "Now, my little tot,
See if the fire is getting hot.
Look inside the oven door
And fan the flame a little more."

But Gretel said, "Please show me how;
You know, I'm just a stupid cow!"

The witch opened the oven wide
And Gretel pushed her right inside.
Hansel and Benjy clapped and cheered,
And just then Bubbles disappeared!

Gretel pushed the witch.
The witch fell in the fire.

Then, Gretel found the witch's key
And set her brother, Hansel, free.

The children looked about and found
Gold and treasure all around.
In every cupboard there were rings,
Necklaces and precious things!

They gathered silver, sweets and gold
As much as each of them could hold.
Then, Benjy with a hop and skip,
Led them on their homeward trip.

The children took some gold.
Then they left the house.

When they got home, the children found
The selfish wife was not around.
Their father cried for joy and kissed them
And told them just how much he'd missed them.

The children made their father rich
And told about the wicked witch.
Then every day was filled with laughter,
And they lived happily ever after.

Hansel and Gretel were home again.

THE END